HERE COMES

MARY ELLEN

By May Justus

Cover illustration by Ecaterina Leascenco

Cover design by Phillip Colhouer

First published in 1940

Illustrated by Helen Finger

This unabridged version has updated grammar and spelling.

© 2019 Jenny Phillips

www.thegoodandthebeautiful.com

Note: Readers should be aware that in the time period this book takes place, many people incorrectly believed in superstitions, even Christians. For example, they believed that dropping a dishrag is a sign of something to come or that picking the very first berries you see of the season brings good luck. The few superstitions that were in this book were taken out because they were made to look real and fulfilled, but we wanted readers to be aware that it was a common practice in those days as it is important to have a correct understanding of history.

To Hope

Who will like to have Mary Ellen
for a book friend

The Circuit Rider brought her to live on Near-Side

Table of Contents

1

Mary Ellen Bakes Bread

Mary Ellen danced down the spring path as if a breeze were behind her, swinging her bucket back and forth to the tune of a ballad song, "The Mill Dam of Binnorie":

"There lived an old lord by the Northern Sea,
    Bow-ee down!
There lived an old lord by the Northern Sea,
    Bow and balance to me,
There lived an old lord by the Northern Sea,
    And he had daughters, one, two, three—"

She had reached the spring now and paused in her song to dip the bucket. Then all of a sudden she straightened, splashing water on her bare feet. A sound of hoofbeats was coming up the creek. A moment later, horse and rider came into sight around the bend.

Mary Ellen caught her breath. Gospel—Old Gospel it was, sure as shooting—and Brother Martin, the Circuit Rider, sitting astraddle of him! She forgot that she was in a hurry to get back with the water. She forgot the stirabout on the fire and the danger that it might burn.

"Howdy, Brother Martin!" she called out as he came nearer.

"Howdy, Mary Ellen! How are ye, Sissy, and how are your folks at home?"

He let his horse's head down to give him a drink. Mary Ellen dipped a gourd full of water and handed it to the preacher man before she answered him. He drank eagerly.

"Much obliged, Sissy—that's the best water this side of the mountain. Been thinking about this spring all the way up the trail. I bet Old Gospel has, too. Much obliged, Sissy," he said again, as he handed back the gourd. "And now we must be on our way to Near-Side."

He tightened his grip on the bridle. Mary Ellen took a step forward.

"But—but—wait, Brother Martin!" It was hard, somehow, to say what she had a mind to say just then. But she was bound to tell him. A chance like this wouldn't come again soon—maybe not for many a day. She got a deep breath and lifted her head, looking at the Circuit Rider squarely.

"Brother Martin, do you *have* to go on to Near-Side tonight?" her voice trembled with eagerness. The Circuit Rider looked at her keenly and answered slowly:

"Well—maybe not—maybe not. Sissy, what's on your mind?"

Mary Ellen got another deep breath and started to tell him. Then all of a sudden she remembered the stirabout which was likely to burn if she didn't get back with water for the pot. But she had a notion, and she gave it words as she picked up the bucket.

"Brother Martin," she said hurriedly, "there *is* something on my mind, but I can't stop here to tell you, or the supper pot will burn certain sure. If you'll ride along—"

"Yes, yes," agreed Brother Martin.

As they went up the path, Mary Ellen told him how she had been hoping for a chance to go to Near-Side. Granny Allen was expecting her to come and stay with her and go to school at the Mission, as she had last year. But it seemed that the chance would never come. Nobody at home could go with her till the fodder pulling was over. They were all at work in the field now—that's why she had been left alone to care for the house and get supper. Her mother had helped with the dinner, but she had gone out with the others to work this afternoon.

"If you could stay all night with us," Mary Ellen wound up her story, "if you could stay till tomorrow and take me with you to Near-Side—it would be a big favor, sure enough! It would, Brother Martin!"

That was the way she had made the trip last year. They had now reached the front-yard gate. The Circuit Rider halted and looked away across the shadowy hollow bordered by the ragged rim of the mountain spur. The sun ball was near to its setting, and in these shortening September days, dusky dark came soon.

"I'll stay the night with you all, I reckon—and thank you kindly, Sissy. It will be a great favor for you to shelter me and my beast."

He went to the stable to put up his horse. Mary
Ellen ran into the kitchen to see about the kettle on
the fire. Thank goodness, it hadn't burned! She set her
wits to work with her hands. She must hurry to finish
the supper. They would all be in from the fodder field
soon—Father, Mother, Big Abe, Ike and Jake, Cissie,
and Tom Tad. Tom Tad was the baby, and no use at all
in the fodder pulling, but he had cried so that they'd
taken him along, riding him piggyback.

It would be hard to leave them after all, to go back
over the mountain to Near-Side, which seemed so far
away from home once she was there. But she wanted
to go in spite of this. She liked to go to school at the
Mission. She liked all the friends she had made on
Near-Side. It had been a wonderful year. And now was
her chance to go back. The Mission school had already
started, but she could study hard and make up all she
had missed. Lovie Lane, her best friend, would help her
too; and Miss Ellison, the teacher, was an understanding sort of person. Miss Ellison knew all about Mary
Ellen's big hope that someday she herself would be a
teacher. That meant she must go on to school for years
and years.

Right now, however, there was something else to do,
and she must hurry. First, she went to the woodpile after
chips and mended the fire. These would burn into coals
very quickly. There should be biscuit bread for supper,
with the Circuit Rider for company, but this she feared

to try. Ash cake she knew how to bake to the satisfaction of the whole family. Even Father said it was good and tasty. Well, she would do her best. In honor of Brother Martin, she would add, maybe, a little shortening. She remembered a crunchy crackling skin rendered for gravy that morning. The very thing to put in!

While the fire burned into glowing embers, she swept the hearth free from ashes, leaving between the andirons a clean bare space on the stone. Then she got the old wooden mixing bowl, sifted yellow meal into it, threw in a pinch of salt, then mixed it with water into a stiff dough. Out of this she made half a dozen fat corn dodgers which she put to bake on the hearthstone in an ash bed heaped high with red hot coals. It would take them about an hour to bake. That would be in good time for supper. The stirabout was already done. She lifted it from the crane and set it on the hearth to keep warm. There ought to be something extra nice for a company supper. Oh, yes, she would set out the honey—or a dish of huckleberry jam. Honey seemed a little more special, she decided, and went to the corner cupboard. It was kept on the very highest shelf, but she could reach it with a chair.

Now her folks were coming home. She heard their talk and laughter, beyond the front-yard gate, and the Circuit Rider greeting them. A welcome guest Brother Martin always was, for he brought them news about people hither and yon, the happenings in outlander places, and many a message sent by kinfolk and friend.

"Mary Ellen baked ash cake on the hearthstone"

Mother came into the kitchen with an anxious face, but she smiled when she saw the preparations which Mary Ellen had already made.

"We'll make out well enough, I reckon," she said, "though I wish we could do better, even on such short notice. Brother Martin's a sensible man—he'll understand the circumstances."

Mary Ellen explained to her mother why she had asked the Circuit Rider to stay all night with them.

"It was a thoughty thing to do," nodded her mother. "You'll be safe in his care on your journey—though I hate to see you go away."

Cissie, who was helping Tom Tad build a corncob house in a corner near the fire, looked up.

"Don't go away, Mary Ellen," she begged.

"Don't—go 'way," echoed the baby.

Mary Ellen choked all of a sudden, "Oh—oh!"

But Mother laughed and spoke up quickly then. "That's no way to talk now! Just think how fine it will be to go on a journey clear to Near-Side! And won't Granny Allen be glad to see you again!"

Granny had come over last spring to make them a visit, but she had soon got so homesick she had gone back to Near-Side.

Big Abe and the twins came in from the barn. Father and the Circuit Rider came in from the dogtrot where they had been laughing and talking away for the last half hour. The shadows of night were deepening fast, and the chill that comes in the mountain after sundown, even in the early fall, drew them all into the comfort of the kitchen room, where a pine-knot fire made warmth and light.

Supper was ready now. They all sat down—all except Mother, who stood up to wait on the table. Brother Martin returned thanks. Then the ash cake and stirabout were passed around.

"Help yourself—take more, Brother Martin," Father kept saying in a mannerly way to their guest.

"There's a plenty—a plenty such as it is," Mother assured him.

Mary Ellen was pleased when the Circuit Rider praised the ash cake, saying that this was his favorite kind of bread.

"My mother used to make it years ago, just so, when I was a boy. Ash cake, when rightly made, is mighty good bread."

It was plain that he meant what he said, too, for he was eating his ash cake as if he enjoyed every bite.

"I'll save a piece," Mary Ellen said, "for a journey cake tomorrow."

"A mighty fine notion," the Circuit Rider said.

2

The Polka-Dot Dresses

Mary Ellen sat in her old place at school by the big glass window and hugged herself with pure joy to be here again. It seemed even better than last year when everything had been new and strange.

How good it was to come back and find it all unchanged: Granny Allen sitting in the dogtrot with the same old greeting, "Howdy, honey, how God loves you!" when she came home every day; Miss Ellison sitting behind her desk with a fresh bouquet each morning, sending a smile out to her as she took her place; and Lovie Lane, a little taller than last year, but the same old Lovie, with her pigtails that wanted to curl and the golden freckles on her face.

And now Mary Ellen felt a nudge from behind and turned in her seat to see Lovie holding out a gaily colored wish book (catalogue) to her.

"It came in the mail," she whispered to her. "And oh," she added, "Mary Ellen, it's plum full of pretty, fine dresses! You never saw the like in all your born days. You never did! They're a wonderly sight to behold!"

Mary Ellen took the catalogue and would have opened

it that minute, but the teacher shook her head to remind her that this was study time. And study just now meant long division. Arithmetic was a cloud in Mary Ellen's sky these days. Spelling now was easy enough, and so was reading. She liked her language work too and could do it very well. But arithmetic—arithmetic was like a riddle to make your head ache. Today, somehow, it took twice as long to get her answers. One thought gladdened her heart. As soon as she had recited it, school would be over, and she and Lovie could look at the wish book on their way homeward.

Granny's cabin

It's a wonder they got home at all that day, that they didn't go in the wrong direction and find themselves at dusky dark on the other side of the mountain. It is a wonder certain sure, for they paid little attention to anything but the wish book which they held in eager hands, walking side by side when they could. And what a sight to behold it was—enough to make a body dizzy, to make one's heart go pit-a-pat, and to put one's head in a whirl! Fine frocks fluttered like pretty butterflies all across the crinkly pages, floweredy, fancy, ruffledy frocks.

"Can any sure-enough clothes be as fine as these, do you reckon?" Mary Ellen asked in wonder.

"Yes," replied Lovie. "The sure-enough dresses are just as pretty as these. You ought to have seen the one Ollie Meyers got last summer—mighty much like a picture in the wish book, it was, I tell you. Blue—morning-glory blue, that was the shade, I remember. And it cost two dollars! I wish I could have a new go-to-meeting dress. But I'd pick a pink one, I think."

"This white one with the polka dots on it is pretty," said Mary Ellen. But she had no hope of ever having a wish-book dress.

The next morning, Lovie met Mary Ellen with a piece of news worth telling.

"Listen, oh, listen, Mary Ellen! I'm to have a new dress, one out of the wish book. My Mammy has promised it to me. She is going to sell a turkey hen to Aunt Malviney Prater and order it for me right away."

"Oh—oh!" exclaimed Mary Ellen. She was glad in truth. She was glad for her friend, but she couldn't help a wishful feeling from filling her heart. Lovie guessed her thoughts.

"Oh, I wish, I *wish*," she cried swiftly, "that you could have a new dress, too! Wouldn't your granny, maybe, order a new dress for you?"

"No," Mary Ellen said in short fashion. She wouldn't because she couldn't just then. Granny Allen had no turkeys or even a spare chicken to sell. She saved eggs up to a dozen and carried them to the store to exchange for the brought-on merchandise they needed.

Mary Ellen's best dress at this time was a rather faded pink gingham. It was still whole with not a patch in it, but the once bright color was dimmer by many washings with homemade soap. She wore this frock on Sunday and on Friday, which was speaking day at school. This was not so bad, she reflected, but to have to wear it to meeting, to see that old pink gingham side by side with Lovie's rosy new dress, this gave her a fairly shamed feeling.

One afternoon not long after this, Mary Ellen went home to find Granny looking through a wish book—a wish book just like Lovie's.

"I got it at the post office," Granny explained. "Nearly all the folks on the mountain have got one. The pictures are a sight for being pretty, but I reckon their looks will come out in the wash." Granny often expressed her suspicions of brought-on goods and store-bought wares. She had more faith in the homespun which she still wove on her old-fashioned loom, in the stockings knit from yarn of her spinning, and in the handcrafts of her mountainside. Sometimes she would buy from a peddler a piece of tinware, a spool of thread, or some little gadget or other, but she nearly always regretted the trade.

"Look out for a peddler's bargain," she often said to warn her neighbors against such temptation.

Mary Ellen knew how Granny felt about newfangled notions, so she did not tell her about Lovie's dress that her mammy was going to order. By and by Granny gave her the wish book, and Mary Ellen kept it as a treasure in the corner of the old chest where she kept her prized possessions. After her lessons were studied each night, she liked to turn the pages and pick out the very prettiest dresses. By her favorite, the blue polka dot, she scribbled "Mary Ellen" and "Lovie" by the pink dress.

And then, three days later, the pink dress came, and Lovie wore it to school to show it off.

"It's pretty for certain," Mary Ellen said again. She would not be stingy with her praises, even if the thought of her old pink gingham made a sort of ache in her bosom.

The accident happened a little later on, in the middle of the writing lesson. Lovie's pen flitted three drops of blue ink and they splattered upon the top ruffle of the skirt of the new dress.

Lovie burst into tears. "Oh, oh, my dress is ruined!

It's ruined, and moreover, Mammy can't get me another, and what will she say when she sees this?"

Mary Ellen tried to console her. "Maybe she can wash it out. I remember one time when Granny soaked an ink spot on my apron in milk, and it came out as good as ever."

"Oh," said Lovie, cheering up a bit. "I believe I will go home with you and ask her to take this out for me. I hate for my Mammy to see it."

But Granny Allen shook her head when she looked at the ink spots later. "I could get the ink spots out all right," she said, "but it would ruin the color of that pink dress. It looks mighty fine, but it won't hold fast in a washing, or I miss my guess. It's brought-on stuff." And Granny's sniff was disdainful.

Lovie began to cry again. She was now more helpless than ever. Then Granny had a bright notion all of a sudden. "I could splatterdash it for you," she said. "We used to wear daub-stick cottons when I was a girl, and we thought them pretty fine. But you'd better go home and ask your mammy if she is willing to have me do that. If she is, you can come back tomorrow, and I'll do my very best for you."

Lovie wiped her eyes and stopped crying. She went away with hope in her heart. After she had gone down the mountain, Granny showed Mary Ellen the way to make splatterdash polka dots. She took a twig of elderberry and chewed one end to make a brush—the daubstick, she told Mary Ellen. This she dipped in a bottle of dye, left from a long-ago dyeing of quilt goods, and touched a scrap of cloth with careful and skillful fingers. The little blue polka dots quickly dried and made a beautiful pattern all over the cloth.

Mary Ellen had a thought, "Oh, Granny, would you mind trying to make my old gingham a polka-dot dress? It wouldn't look half so faded if it had polka dots all over it. It would look a little like the picture."

"What picture?" Granny asked.

"In the wish book," answered Mary Ellen, and she ran to get it.

Granny Allen looked. Granny Allen studied the picture for a minute or two. "That dress is white," she murmured, as if she were talking all to herself. "We will bleach that gingham before we put the polka dots on."

And this is the way she did it, with Mary Ellen on hand to help. They put the dress in a kettle of hot water with some lye soap and boiled it until all the faded color came out and the dress was white. Then it had to be dried and pressed nicely. Mary Ellen could hardly wait. At last the dress was ready for the polka dots, and Granny put on some of them. She thought it great fun to do this. When the dress was all covered with polka dots, it was pressed out nicely again.

"It looks," cried Mary Ellen, "just like a new dress, Granny! It is as pretty as the one in the wish book, I think."

Granny agreed. "Yes, I reckon it is. And it'll wear you a sight better. I'll set the dots fast in the cloth on the first washing day."

3

Neighbors for the Night

The sun had slipped out of sight behind Piney Point, and dusk lay like a shawl around the shoulder of Near-Side-And-Far.

In Granny Allen's cabin, the hearth fire leaped and laughed at the creeping shadows as if daring them to come in at the door, which was not yet shut for the night.

A late October evening is always chilly in the mountains, though the day behind it may have been warm. Just as soon as the sun dips from view, night comes apace like a swift-stepping giant from the hollows, eager to enter his rugged dominion and rule till break o' day.

Mary Ellen piled chips on the fire. These would make coals in a hurry, and Granny was even now sifting meal to bake for their supper bread. The oven sat on a bed of coals, and the oven lid was heating in the crackling flame of the cheery fire.

"You might grease the oven," Granny said, as Mary Ellen kept turning around and about on the heels and toes. Mary Ellen flew to the cupboard to get a piece of bacon rind, but she was interrupted right in the middle of a hop and skip.

"Howdy!" called a voice through the doorway.

Granny went forward, bread bowl in hand, Mary Ellen pressing in behind her. They had not replied to the call from the dark, for it was the voice of a stranger. The face was that of a stranger, too, a strange man, but not an outlander. This was a mountain man, they could tell right away. No, this was no outlander person.

"Howdy," said Granny hospitably. "Come in." But the man did not accept her invitation, though the cabin door was swung wide now.

"No, thanks to you," was the answer spoken in a mannerly way. "We are North Carolina people peddling apples down here in Tennessee on our way to see my wife's people. We camp out at night and cook our food, but the baby is sort o' puny, and I'd like to get a little milk for him if you have it to spare," he ended.

"We can spare you some," Granny said at once. "Sit down while I fix it for you." She took the tin bucket the man held out and handed it to Mary Ellen.

"Give him half the supper milk," she whispered. "I'd just as soon have sop gravy." And so Mary Ellen went to pour the milk. Half the supper milk seemed so very little. She poured her share into the bucket, too. She couldn't say she liked sop gravy as well as fresh sweet milk. No, she didn't—but then one must manage for a baby, especially a puny baby, she thought.

The man took the milk and offered to pay for it, but Granny refused.

"Just a neighborly turn," she told him, "and you are our neighbors for the night, though you hail from North Caroliny."

Now the oven was greased, and the fat corn dodgers were popped inside for baking. While they waited for the bread to be done, they talked of the apple-wagon people camping below them in the gap.

"They might be our own kin-people," Granny said. "They are McIntyres, and we have some McIntyre relations."

"I'd like to see the baby," said Mary Ellen, thinking of her own little brother, Tom Tad, back home. Her arms just ached to hold a baby!

Perhaps Granny guessed how she felt just then, and perhaps Granny, too, felt a longing to hold a baby. For she said right away, as if by sudden inspiration, "I have a notion for the two of us to go and pay a neighborly visit to the McIntyres after supper tonight."

Mary Ellen was filled with excitement and joy to think of this little trip.

"I wish I had a present for the baby," she said almost to herself. But Granny Allen overheard her.

"A kind thought, honey, but it seems to me that you've made a gift to the baby. You sent your supper milk to him, I know. I saw you fill the bucket."

But they found something to take along. Granny got a honeysuckle basket and put in a fat corn pone, still warm, left from their evening meal. A pat of fresh butter went along with this and a jar of muscadine jelly.

"No fancy fixing," Granny said, "but it always seemed to me that neighborly kindness flavors food."

"I want to carry something," Mary Ellen wished aloud. Then, all of a sudden, a notion came into her head.

"I know—the yarn dolly!" She had made it for her little brother, but there would be plenty of time to make another doll before she went home.

The McIntyres had a cheerful campfire close to their apple wagon, and they seemed pleased to have visitors.

"Sit down and make yourselves at home," Mrs. McIntyre said right after the first words of greeting. For chairs there were upturned bushel measures. Mary Ellen chose a handy stump.

"Come on, Buddie," Mrs. McIntyre called, raising her voice a little, and then she laughed. "Buddie is bashful. This is his first trip away from home."

Buddie, a boy about a head higher than Mary Ellen, slipped shyly into the wavering circle of light.

"Mind your manners," his father said when he did not answer to Granny's "Howdy, son!" Then Buddie answered, "Howdy!" and backed into the shadows again. He crept out a little later and made shy talk with Mary Ellen, while the grown folks were gossiping away and paying no attention to them. By this time Mary Ellen had the baby and was having a fine time with him, dancing the yarn dolly up and down before his eyes. The baby was something to talk about, Mary Ellen and Buddie discovered. Jackie was his name, a very nice baby, almost as nice as Tom Tad had been.

"I made a pretty today," Buddie said, "while I was riding in the wagon." He pulled it from his pocket and held it out: a leather string full of buckeyes—buckeyes carved into funny faces. Mary Ellen admired it. "Keep it if you like," Buddie said.

"But they found something to take along..."

"Many thanks," Mary Ellen answered, "but I hate to take it from you. There's a sight of pretty work on it."

"Oh, it's nothing," the boy said. "Take it along for a keepsake. I've heard tell it is a good thing to keep a gift a new friend gives you."

"Many thanks," Mary Ellen said.

The baby was asleep now, and again his mother came to take him.

"Buddie!" his father called to him. "Go bring us a basket of apples. Pick out some of the different kinds—I want our friends to sample them."

Mary Ellen went along, too, to help Buddie carry the basket. Such beautiful apples! So many kinds, even Buddie didn't know the names of all of them. Winesaps, rusty coats, and Ben Davis were all familiar.

"I like to roast 'em on a stick," Buddie said.

"I never did that," Mary Ellen said, "but I've roasted them before the hearthfire."

"I like 'em on a stick," said Buddie, and he showed Mary Ellen how to roast an apple this way.

"Something I like is candy apples," Mr. McIntyre told them. "What about a little treat, Mother?" His wife smiled over at him.

"We've plenty of molasses, if you can spare a bucket to boil the candy in," she said.

"I'll find one," Buddie cried, and he dashed off to return with one. Soon the candy was cooking on the coals, bubbling and boiling away, and the air was sweet with the smell of it. The fire was hot. The candy cooked quickly. Mrs. McIntyre tried it with a splinter.

"It's just right, now," she said.

Buddie was ready with an apple on a stick, but he remembered his manners this time without being told.

"You're first, Mary Ellen," he said, and he showed her how to dip her apple in and then to cool it a little by waving it around in the air for a long minute or two. Then it was candy on the outside. The first bite was delicious, and the next was better. Granny liked her candy apple, too, though it took her nearly twice as long as the other folks to eat it, for she had only a few teeth, and these did not match very well.

An hour later Mary Ellen and Granny went back to their cabin, leaving their friends to their campfire. They hoped to see them again next year in apple time.

"They are neighborly folks," said Granny. She had a basket of fine apples and Mary Ellen the string of buckeyes for a keepsake. Buddy had said they were special.

4

Many a Mile to Go

It was corn-pulling time on Near-Side, and the school had a week's vacation. Mary Ellen ought to have been happy, but she didn't seem happy—not a mite.

Something was the matter with Mary Ellen. Granny saw that she was looking donsie and began to dose her liberally with pennyroyal tea. But for all her dosing, Mary Ellen showed mighty little improvement and went about like a droopy chick.

"What ails you, honey?" Granny would say. "Do you feel a pain inside of you?"

"No, Granny," Mary Ellen would answer, "I don't hurt anywhere at all." Then she would run out and play or set herself to some task just to show Granny Allen that she was all right. But she wasn't, not quite. Mary Ellen was wanting to go home to Far-Side and see her folks, so she was sick after a fashion—homesick—but she was ashamed to let on. A whole month had gone by since the Circuit Rider, Brother Martin, had brought her to live on Near-Side and go to the Mission school. She liked to live with Granny Allen. She liked it better than last year, but she couldn't help missing her homefolks.

She wanted to see them all again: Father, Mother, Big Abe, the twins, Cissie, and her little brother, Tom Tad. Dilly wouldn't be there, of course. She had married and moved away from Far-Side last year. But she could see all the others if she could manage a visit home some of these days.

As she thought of this, she sighed so loud that Granny Allen heard her and looked up from her quilt piecing.

"You got a cold in your head, honey?"

"No," Mary Ellen managed to answer, and she grabbed the chip basket and ran outside. She was obliged to do something, and right away, too, or she couldn't keep from crying.

As she opened the door, she ran against a person who was standing outside it with his hand raised up ready to knock.

Bump! Thud! Crash! "Hey—hey!" cried a voice. It was Step-Along, the peddler, who carried his pack up and down the trails. He was always in a great hurry.

"I've got to step along," he would always say when he was invited to tarry, and this is how he got his name. If he had another, nobody knew it.

Now he picked up, with Mary Ellen's help, the few things that he had scattered, chuckling good-naturedly all the while. The only thing in any way injured was a tin wash pan which had rolled across the porch and landed in the yard, getting a dent somewhere on the way. But Step-Along said it was no matter.

They entered the house to Granny's call, "Come

"She would set herself to some task just to show Granny she was all right"

in—come in this minute! The wind blows the smoke every which away!"

She was glad to see the peddler. He carried a great deal more than the big pack of wares—Step-Along carried friendly gossip about all the folks on Near-Side-And-Far. He carried word from neighbor to neighbor and sometimes a letter as well. He was an accommo-dating person, as you may guess. Granny welcomed him, though she had no mind to buy anything from his pack today.

"No needles, no pins, no calico, or shiny buttons?" Step-Along asked as he showed her his wares.

Granny shook her head. "It is nothing that I can buy today," she said. "But don't be in a hurry to go," she added in a mannerly way. "It is nearly time for dinner."

Step-Along said, "No." He said it three times, but the truth is he was very hungry, and he had many a mile to go. Of course, Granny Allen insisted and, in the end, Step-Along stayed.

Mary Ellen helped get the dinner and listened while Step-Along told all the news. He had stayed all night with Mary Ellen's family a week ago. They were all well. And Tom Tad was riding a horse with one of the twins to hold him on!

"Oh, I *wish* I could go home and see him!" Mary Ellen cried.

"Why don't you, then?" Step-Along turned and asked her. "I'm bound for Far-Side. Go along with me."

Mary Ellen looked over at Granny. She would hate

to leave the old woman all by herself. Granny guessed what she was thinking.

"I could stay at night with a neighbor," she said, "to keep from feeling lonely. Go along, Mary Ellen, if you like."

"Could I be back for school on Monday?" Mary Ellen asked. She must not miss school. But Step-Along reassured her, "I'll be back this way come Saturday."

"Oh, goody!" Mary Ellen shouted.

She could hardly eat any of the dinner herself because she was so excited, and Step-Along said that he got her share of succotash and sweet potatoes.

When they were almost ready to start, Mary Ellen thought of something. "I wish that I had a present for them—for *all* of them," she added.

"Here," said Step-Along, "I've got to pay for my dinner, and since I ate your share, too, I reckon this belongs to you."

The wash pan! The shiny new pan with only one little dent in it, and nobody would mind that a bit. A wash pan! They could all use it, so it would be a present for all. And their old wash pan was rusty and leaked in half a dozen holes.

"It's the very thing!" said Mary Ellen. "Won't they all be tickled over this?"

"Let's get started," said the peddler. "We'd better step along, I say. It's a pretty long trail across the mountain, and we've many a mile to go."

Step-Along

5

Here Comes Mary Ellen

Big Abe caught sight of Mary Ellen and Step-Along, the peddler, coming down the rocky trail of Far-Side. He had started to call the pigs for their evening meal, "Pig—o—ee!—Pig—!" But he broke off to yell to the homefolks, "Here comes Mary Ellen!" And everybody rushed through the door: Father, Mother, the twins, Ike and Jake, Cissie, and Tom Tad—they all ran to meet her.

"Here she comes!"

"Have you come home to stay, Mary Ellen?"

"Do you have to go back?"

"Is Granny all right?"

These and many other questions they asked as they crowded all around. Mary Ellen did her best to tell the whys and wherefores of her coming home.

"They are having a week's vacation in the Mission school on Near-Side. I found out that Step-Along was coming to Far-Side, so I came along with him. School opens up again on Monday, so I have to go back Saturday."

"Well! Well, I say!" cried Mother. "Let's all go in and settle ourselves. I declare I feel nearly addled with all this excitement. You come, too," she said to the peddler, remembering her manners belatedly.

"No, much obliged," the peddler said politely. "I'll just be stepping along, I reckon. I'll be back to see you all later."

"He had started to call the pigs..."

No doubt he realized that this was no time for a peddler to try to sell any of his wares. Nobody here had any attention for anything or anybody but Mary Ellen, who had been away from home—clear across the mountain. There was much to ask and much to tell. While Mother got supper, she told them all about Near-Side. Most of all she talked about school.

"I sit by a glass window as I did last year," she proudly said. "And even in bad weather, you can see what is going on outside."

Big Abe turned around to his father, "Let's get a window when we sell the pigs."

"We might do that," was the answer.

Ike and Jake clapped their hands and said, "We're going to have a glass window!"

"Maybe so," Father said. He didn't sound sure, for certain, but it was a bright hope anyway.

By that time supper was ready—fried chicken and hot biscuit bread, a real company supper, Mary Ellen thought. Cissie ate by her. Her quiet little sister smiled shyly at her now and then.

"I've brought you something," Mary Ellen whispered. She had made up her mind to give her little sister the precious chinquapin necklace which Lovie Lane had given her and which she was still wearing.

After supper Father and the boys shelled corn for the next day's milling—the first new bread corn of that year.

"It's a mite sappy," Father said, "but the old corn's out, so we'll make this do."

"It'll bake up fine," said Mother.

In the pine-knot firelight, Mary Ellen made a corncob pen for the baby to knock over. Tom Tad had certainly grown. He would soon be big enough to go to the mill by himself, Father bragged, making a joke to tickle everybody.

"What have you learned in school, Mary Ellen?" Big Abe asked.

"A lot o' things," she replied. "I can read a whole lot better than I could last year. I've read a lot of books," she told him.

"Read us some then," challenged one of the twins.

"Yes, let's hear you read," said the other, as if he had his doubts about it.

"Read what?" asked Mary Ellen, smiling a little at their curiosity.

"The Bible," suggested Mother. "But maybe that has too many hard words."

"I will read the Shepherd Psalm," said Mary Ellen. And she did while they listened respectfully.

"I've got another notion," said Father. "Read me a page in the almanac, and see what kind of weather we're going to have along about Thanksgiving." It was then that they always butchered their hogs and made the lard and sausage, the liver puddings, and crackling bread. Mary Ellen read about the weather from the almanac, and Father was pleased, for it promised a freeze. A good time for hog killing, for then the meat would be sure to keep.

By and by Cissie thought of something.

"Can you write as well as you can read, Mary Ellen?" she asked her in a whisper.

Big Abe overheard and laughed.

"Don't you be getting Mary Ellen to write your love letters now," he teased.

Cissie laughed, but her fair cheeks reddened. Mary Ellen squeezed Cissie's hand.

"I'll write you a letter," she promised. "I've learned to write very good letters, I think. In our English exercises, we have to write a letter every week."

"You're a sight smart," Cissie told her. Reading and writing were somewhat of a mystery to her.

By this time the new corn shelling was all done. Father sacked the corn. The boys piled the cobs in a corner to be used as fuel. A corncob fire is a fine quick one for cooking.

Now that work was out of the way, it was time for a little pleasure making. Big Abe took down his banjo from the wall and thumbed a few chords. Mary Ellen recognized her favorite tune, "Down in the Valley." She began to hum it, and Big Abe cried, "Sing it out. Sing it out, Mary Ellen!" And Mary Ellen sang from memory these words of the old, old ballad:

"*Down in the valley, the valley so low,*
Hang your head downward, hear the wind blow.
Hear the wind blow, dear, hear the wind blow.
Hang your head downward, hear the wind blow."

Just as she finished the first stanza, a sudden gale shrieked around the corner, rattling the door and wooden window shutters. A smoke cloud swept across the room from the chimney mouth.

"Falling weather soon," spoke Father from his corner. "A certain-sure sign when the smoke leaps out." There was too much coughing and sneezing for any more singing just then. Besides, Mary Ellen felt sleepy. It had been a long time since she had woken up on the other side at Granny Allen's—and here she was back in her old home!

The trundle bed was ready for her. She was going to sleep beside Cissie, who was already there and nearly asleep.

"Come on, Mary Ellen," she whispered. "There's plenty of room for both of us."

Mary Ellen crept in beside her sister and made herself a nest in the fat featherbed.

"It's good to come home," said Mary Ellen.

6

Mary Ellen's Featherbed

It was still autumn by the calendar because it was still November, but winter was hurrying on his way up Near-Side-And-Far. Mary Ellen followed a frozen trail on her way to school these mornings, swinging her arms to keep warm and skipping to limber up her toes. Yes, another winter was here. Granny Allen had prophesied it a good while back.

"We'll have an early winter this year. The wasps are building low to the ground."

All through the summer season they had made ready. The dugout under the kitchen floor was heaped with turnips and potatoes. The rafters of the cabin kitchen were hung with long strips of dried apples, pumpkin rings, and shucky beans. On the high shelf of the corner cupboard were jars of apple butter, huckleberry jam, and wild honey. Uncle Tobe had given them a share of the treasure found in a bee tree up on Piney Point, and this they had saved for special days or when they had company.

Mary Ellen had new red mittens which Granny had made for her, and soon she would have a new red cap which Granny was knitting to match. Mary Ellen had new shoes, very black and shiny, bought by Granny with many a dozen of her Dominicker hen's eggs.

"You are so good to me," Mary Ellen often said to thank Granny Allen. "I do wish that I had a chance to do a good turn for you."

One day Mary Ellen, coming home from school, found a caller at their cabin—Step-Along, the peddler man, with his pack in the middle of the floor. It was untied, and all around was spilled its colorful store of bright cloth, gay ribbons, shiny pans, and glittering trinkets. Granny bought a paper of needles.

"Something else, something more," Step-Along kept urging her. "Now here is something pretty. Wouldn't that make you a fine go-to-meeting dress?"

And it was a sight to behold, the piece of cloth he held up, a gray that was almost blue, like the shadow of midsummer dusk or the haze of Indian summer.

"Yes, it's a pretty fine dress pattern," Granny Allen was saying, "too fine for me." But she asked the price.

"Just three dollars," replied the peddler.

Granny shook her head. "No," she said, "it's too high. I haven't so much as a dollar."

Step-Along was an old acquaintance, so Granny didn't mind telling the truth to him. Step-Along looked sad. He did like to drive a bargain, and he wanted Granny to have the pretty dress. Step-Along had a notion.

"I'll let you have it on credit," he said. "You can pay me when you are able."

But Granny wouldn't listen to this. "Debt is a hard taskmaster, and one I have never served," she said.

Mary Ellen sighed as the peddler put the cloth away and tied up his big bundle. How she wished that she had some money tucked away, a little hidden treasure which she could now bring out to buy this go-to-meeting dress for Granny! It was late in the day now, and dark was pushing his way up the spur of the mountain. Mary Ellen heaped chips on the fire to make a cheerful blaze and burn into coals for the oven lid. It would soon be time for breadmaking. Granny was a hospitable soul. She invited Step-Along to stay and share the evening meal with them. The peddler had his bundle already on his shoulder, his face was turned to the open door, but he agreed to stay after he had been asked three times.

"I reckon I'll tarry," he answered and shifted the big pack into a corner where it would be out of the way.

Mary Ellen was glad that Step-Along was going to stay for supper. She was always fond of company, no matter who it might be—the schoolteacher, the Circuit Rider, the peddler man, or a neighbor. Mary Ellen, helping Granny get the supper, listened happily to the pleasant talk. The meal was ready soon: corn pone and milk and butter, and a bit of wild honey for dessert, since Step-Along was company.

After supper Step-Along said to them, "I'll be moving along, I reckon," but at the door, he stopped in the face of a gust of wind and rain. The window shutter rattled; the rafters creaked.

"It's coming up a storm," said Granny. "I'm not surprised, for I noticed all day the way the smoke trailed the ground. You can't go out on the mountain tonight. Stay with us. I will lay you a pallet up in the loft room."

Step-Along stayed. All this pleased Mary Ellen, for Step-Along had a tireless tongue. He could tell a tale or sing an old ballad whenever he had the notion in his head—and tonight he beat himself for certain.

When bedtime drew on, Granny leaned over and whispered to Mary Ellen, "Will you let Step-Along have your featherbed to use tonight for a pallet? It is cold in the loft room. A straw tick will hardly keep him from freezing."

"Yes," Mary Ellen agreed at once. So the goose featherbed was taken into the loft room for Step-Along's pallet. Mary Ellen herself slept warmly on the straw tick in her corner by the fire. She hardly missed the feathers because the trundle bed was heaped with blankets and bright quilted patchwork covers. With the half-remembered lines of some old ballad songs going over and over in her head, Mary Ellen fell asleep. The wild wind danced around the corners of the little cabin singing its wild song, but Mary Ellen did not hear it.

When she woke, Step-Along and Granny were already having breakfast, and Step-Along's tongue was rattling away.

"It's a wonder I woke up this morning, I slept so sound. Been a mighty long time since I have slept on feathers. Best bed I ever saw in my life. You wouldn't sell it to me, I reckon?"

This was a joke, of course, Mary Ellen knew, but all at once she had a notion, and she turned it around and around in her head to see if it was good for something.

After their company had gone, Mary Ellen helped Granny Allen put everything in the house to rights. She knew how to spread the covers just so and how to punch up the big fat pillows. She always made up her own bed, and sometimes she helped with Granny's. This morning, however, Granny made her own bed, and when she picked up a pillow to put it in place, she had a surprise.

"My soul and body! Look-a-here!"

But Mary Ellen didn't need to look. She knew what Granny was seeing with wondering, astonished, delighted eyes.

"The go-to-meeting dress he left for me!" Then she shook her head sadly. "I can't keep it. I can't keep it, Mary Ellen. I can't keep a dress that I can't pay for."

"I have paid for it," Mary Ellen told Granny Allen. She said it a little proudly, and then she went on to tell the whole tale.

"I made a bargain," she said, "with Step-Along before he left. He's to stay at our house this winter one night a month, and every night he's to sleep on my featherbed!"

"Then she went on to tell the whole tale..."

7

Better Than Huckleberry Pie

One Saturday morning Granny Allen said, "We'd better cook extra for dinner, for I feel someone might be coming for dinner."

"Are you certain sure?" asked Mary Ellen.

"Certain sure enough," answered Granny. "We'll be on the safe side anyway, if we cook another handful of beans." So saying, she dumped them into the pot and set it to swinging on the big crane hook above the fire. It takes a long time for shucky beans to cook right. When they don't get done, they are just as tough as leather. Mary Ellen piled some chips on the fire just beneath the pot, and soon a bubbling singsong told that the bean pot was cooking. Later on, there would be a brown pone of cornmeal crackling bread baked in the three-legged oven on the hearth. The cracklings were a gift from Aunt Hannah, who had more than she could use herself from her lard making yesterday.

A busy day was ahead of them, for Granny and Mary Ellen had planned to daub their house today. The clay chinking in the wall was loose in places, and there were many cracks through which the winter wind could find its way. They had planned for a long time to get to the job, and this was the very day to do it. Uncle Tobe had given them a lot of hog bristles, and there was fine mud for mixing at the chicken pond nearby, for it had rained the first of the week. It was a messy task, to be sure, but Mary Ellen didn't mind it. Of course, it wasn't quite as easy as it was to make mud pies, but she liked to feel the soft, wet clay, to squeeze it with her fingers, and to slap and pat it into place. The bristles made it hold together after it was daubed into the chinking of the walls.

They were right in the middle of their work when the big surprise happened. Clop! Clop! They heard a horse as it crossed No-End Creek; a minute later, they saw the rider.

"It's Abe!" cried Mary Ellen, jumping up and scattering mud every which aways.

Abe it was. He got down from his horse and would have hugged Mary Ellen, mud and all, if Granny hadn't cried, "Go wash yourself first, child. Abe will ruin that go-to-meeting suit if he gets within three feet of you. I can't make out to shake hands, Grandson, but I bid a kind welcome to you."

When Mary Ellen came back, her brother, Abe, was telling how he had been to a play frolic far down No-End Creek. He was riding home this way for a chance to see Mary Ellen and Granny, too, and to find out how they were getting along.

Mary Ellen saw that he had his banjo hitched across his saddle and asked right away if he would take time to play them a ballad song.

"'Down in the Valley,' maybe," she suggested, and Big Abe winked and laughed at her.

"Maybe I've forgotten it," he teased. He knew it was her favorite song. Mary Ellen laughed and made no reply. She knew he had not forgotten.

"I'll play it for you, by and by, I reckon. But most times when I play away from home, folks pay me back in some way or another. Last night they made me all the candy that I could eat."

"I never made candy," Mary Ellen said, "but I can make you something nearly as good."

"What's that?" asked Abe.

It was huckleberry pie that Mary Ellen had in mind, but she decided not to tell him. It would be a heap nicer, she thought, to have it for a surprise. She had never made a pie at home.

"If you will stay for dinner, I'll show you what it is," she said.

"Stay, Grandson," urged Granny. "There's plenty enough for dinner."

A few minutes later, Abe stuck his head inside the kitchen door.

"Don't be snooping, now," Mary Ellen said.

"I'm not," Big Abe assured her. "I want to find an old pair of overalls that I left here last year. I'm going to help Granny awhile."

"They're in the loft room," said Mary Ellen. "I saw them there last summer under an old gable rafter, hanging on a peg."

Soon he was out of the house again, and Mary Ellen went about her dinner. First, she set the oven on the hearth and made the crackling bread. While it baked, she would make the pie. But alas for her fine intentions! There was no flour in the bin. And how could you make a pie without flour? It couldn't be done.

Mary Ellen felt like crying. Then she thought, "I can borrow some flour from Aunt Hannah." She could slip up the trail to her house—it was not a very long way—and be back again in no time at all. Soon she was fairly flying on the way with a light heart.

"May I borrow some flour to make a pie for Abe, Aunt Hannah?" she asked as soon as she got to the door, her legs nearly giving way, she was so tired.

Aunt Hannah shook her head regretfully. "I made the last dust of flour for breakfast, and Tobe won't be back with a turn till some time late in the day."

Mary Ellen's hopes fell.

"Why don't you make a huckleberry pudding instead of a huckleberry pie?" Aunt Hannah asked. "You have cornmeal, I reckon."

"Yes," nodded Mary Ellen.

"Eggs and milk?"

"Yes," she nodded again.

"Any molasses?"

"Yes, we have some molasses." She could use what was in the pitcher.

"You can make the pudding," Aunt Hannah said, and she told her just how it was done.

Down the trail again on flying feet, she remembered the bread in the oven. Oh, how she hoped that the crackling bread would not be burned. She hoped, too, that she hadn't been missed.

A single glance around the corner showed her Granny and Abe at work, and since they were working on the far end of the house now, they paid no attention to her as she slipped into the kitchen. The crackling bread was not burned—just a beautiful dark brown crust. Now she could put the pudding on.

"Down the trail again on flying feet..."

"Scald one cup of cornmeal in a quart of milk," she whispered to herself as if it were a speech that she was trying to learn.

"Add two eggs and a half-cup of sorghum molasses— and what—oh, a smidgen of salt, and last of all, a cup of huckleberries."

Oh, yes, she had it all learned! She was glad to know that she could remember.

Soon the pudding was baking. She could hardly wait till it was done so that she could call them in. She would put it in the middle of the table and watch Abe's face when his eyes fell upon it.

"It's mighty nigh dinnertime by the hollow feeling inside of me," said Big Abe looking through the doorway a little later. Mary Ellen was setting the table.

"I reckon I'll have dinner on by the time you and Granny get washed up." She had just peeped in at the pudding, and it was beginning to look and smell as if it were getting done.

Abe went down to the creek to clean up and left the wash basin to Granny.

"What is it that smells so good?" she asked.

"And looks so good?" Abe was gazing at the fragrant, steamy dish that Mary Ellen was placing in the middle of the table.

"Huckleberry pudding," Mary Ellen explained. It was a very proud moment, but a prouder one it was when Big Abe remarked as he took his third helping, "Huckleberry pudding, I do believe, is better than huckleberry pie."

8

The Rising Sun

Granny Allen had taken advantage of a pleasant spell of late fall weather to get a certain piece of quilting done. Through all the spring and summertime, she had been busy in her garden and truck patches about the house. But now the autumn had come, and her little crop was harvested. Mary Ellen had helped her gather the corn, the pumpkins, the potatoes, the peas, the peppers, and the beans. These good things were safely stored away to last them through the long winter. Some of the precious store was hidden in the dugout beneath the floor. Some of it hung above their heads from the smoke-darkened rafters of the kitchen. It was good to know they had so much.

Today she and Mary Ellen had swung the quilting frames in the dogtrot, for Granny liked to sit with her back in a patch of sun. It helped her rheumatism, she said, and she needed a good light for quilting. Granny Allen took great pride in her work. Her old fingers were slow, but her stitching was still even and fine as she followed the Spider Web pattern on this new cover she had made. It was a mighty pretty "kivver," as Granny

Allen called it. "The Rising Sun"—what a pretty name! And what a pretty color, too, Mary Ellen thought as she looked down at it. The sun rays were such a bright yellow. And oh, how many there were! Big rays and little rays. Mary Ellen thought all of a sudden that she would like to count the little pieces in one quilt block.

"A hundred and eighty-five!" she announced a few minutes later.

"You counted right," Granny Allen said. "But that's just the number in *one* quilt block. How many in *all*?"

She looked up, but Mary Ellen shook her head. "That's too hard to count. It's like an arithmetic problem. I could work it out on my slate, maybe."

"Nine times a hundred and eighty-five. There are nine big blocks as you can see. Maybe you think it's hard to count 'em! What if you sat down to make the kivver?"

Again Mary Ellen shook her head. "I'll never be as smart as you, Granny," she declared in a rather hopeless voice.

Granny Allen laughed. "That sounds like me about three score years ago. You'll learn, honey, you'll learn," she said. "You've already made a Nine Patch, and you can sew very well. Your stitches are nice and neat, and you are improving, too. My first quilt was pieced in a Candlelight pattern, and it went every which way. It was pieced by candlelight, too. 'Patience Corners' it was called, a good name for it."

Mary Ellen stood by Granny Allen's side to admire the quilt a little longer.

"Granny...had taken advantage of a pleasant spell of fall weather
to get some quilting done"

"Which bed will you put it on?" she asked. Oh, if Granny should spread it on hers! But Granny was looking at her with a sly twinkle.

"Can you keep a secret?"

"Yes, Granny, oh, yes, I can!"

"Then I'll tell you something. This quilt is to go to a faraway place—New York City. The Mission teacher has an order for it. She told me about it one day when I went down to take her some eggs. She knows about a shop in New York City where they sell handmade things, and she got the order for me."

"Oh, Granny—and you hadn't said a word about it!"

Granny laughed. "I said it was a secret. I wanted to surprise you—a big surprise—when the money came for the quilt."

"Money!" cried Mary Ellen. "How much? How much, Granny?"

"Twenty-five dollars!" Granny whispered, as if it took her breath just to think of it.

"It seems too good to be true, Granny. I wish I could help you, but I'd be afraid to put a stitch in 'The Rising Sun.' I guess I'll just have to help you by doing extra turns at the housework so that you can have more time to quilt," Mary Ellen said.

For a week longer they had warm, pleasant weather. Indian summer lingered late that year on the slope of Near-Side.

"It won't last," Granny Allen kept saying. "Winter's just around the corner, but before the bad weather comes, I want to get this quilt done."

She knew that she could not see to quilt the delicate design inside the dark little cabin.

"Only one more block," she said one day as she put up her needle and thimble when the light had grown too dim for her to follow the pattern any longer. Then she looked away toward the barnyard where she heard a rooster crowing.

"Run and see if the chickens have gone to roost," she bade Mary Ellen. "If they have gone to roost this early in the day, it's a sure sign of changing weather."

Mary Ellen skipped off and was soon back to say that the chickens had gone to bed early, and the old rooster continued to crow.

"It's a sure sign," repeated Granny. Then she quoted the old weather sign:

> "If a rooster crows when he goes to bed,
> He's sure to get up with a very wet head."

They took down "The Rising Sun" that night and swung it inside the cabin where it would be safe from falling weather. And a good thing they did, for that night a wild wind blew up from No-End Hollow and, sweeping across the mountain, left behind it a whole week of sleet and rain.

Mary Ellen and Granny were weatherbound. No going to school in such weather—it was impossible, for all the trails were little creeks by now. They had to keep the window shutters tight and the door fast bolted. The only light was the pine-knot fire that danced upon the hearth. By it, Granny knitted and Mary Ellen read the stories out of her reader. Granny liked to hear these and praised Mary Ellen for reading them so well. Sometimes they sang some old ballad songs. It might be "Barbara Allen," "The Golden Vanity," or "Fair Ellender." Mary Ellen liked these old songs, and singing helped to pass the time away. But even so, the days went slowly. Granny worried because she couldn't get the rest of her quilting done. A corner of the quilt was still unfinished. If only it could be ready to send down to the Mission when some neighbor passed along. The order was long overdue. Besides, Granny wanted the money to buy some things they needed now and would need more with winter coming on.

It was all this worry, no doubt, that helped to put Granny in bed—that and a sudden sharp attack of her old foe, rheumatism. Mary Ellen made her pots of strong herb tea and kept her warm in bed by heating rocks to put to her feet. More days passed, and then clear weather—clear weather, but cold it was, cold enough to freeze your nose if you didn't warm it while outdoors by rubbing it with a finger.

Then here came Step-Along one day. He was on his way to the Mission. What a chance to send the quilt! If only that corner were done!

"I'm in no great hurry," said Step-Along, who hoped to be asked for dinner. "Couldn't you finish it right away and let me take it?"

"It's too dark in here to quilt," Granny said, "and besides, my hands are so crippled that I couldn't quilt a line to save my life."

Mary Ellen had a notion. She tried to keep it to herself till she thought it over twice—but it would not keep any longer.

"Let me quilt the last corner, Granny. *Please* let me quilt it!" she cried. "I will be so careful. I have already learned how to make little stitches—you said so yourself one day not long ago."

Granny took a long minute to decide. "I reckon you could try," she said at last. "It's our one chance to get it to the Mission any time soon."

Mary Ellen left Step-Along to mind the fire and to keep an eye on the dinner—shucky beans, swinging on the crane, and sweet potatoes in the ashes. She opened the window shutter just a crack, then settled down to her quilting. Oh, how hard she tried to do it well! The work was very slow, for she took a great deal of pains with it. She forgot all about the dinner. She paid no attention to the talk that went on. Stitch, stitch, she kept on and on.

"Dinner's ready!" the peddler cried at last. She looked up to see it on the table. He had fixed it all by himself. The beans and potatoes were on a little stand near Granny's bed.

"I wanted to help," the peddler told her. After dinner, he washed up while Mary Ellen stitched away on the last lines of the spider web pattern. And now the very last was finished!

"Look! Look!" Mary Ellen cried. "Look at 'The Rising Sun'!" The peddler came over and looked down to see. Granny sat up in bed to view it while Mary Ellen widened the shutter to let more light come in.

"Fine work, fine work!" said Step-Along.

"Pretty fine work," approved Granny. "I reckon you'll have to help me get a start on making *you* a 'Rising Sun'!"

9

Christmas Gift

It was drawing near to Christmas time down at Near-Side Mission, and the children were making merry with all their Christmas plans. First and foremost in importance was the wonderful Christmas Eve program in which everybody had a part. There was a play this year and many carols and speeches besides, a truly wonderful program.

And other fun was on hand, too. Fun better than any game or play was the making of Christmas presents these days. Miss Ellison, the teacher, let them make presents every afternoon. They were making a lot of things: pincushions, pot holders, work bags, and pillow covers. These were the presents made by the girls. The boys made other things: tops, toy furniture, hearth brooms, and match holders. As they worked away, they made many plans and talked them over and over. Mary Ellen and Lovie Lane often put their heads together and shared their secrets with each other.

"This pincushion is for Mammy."

"This pot holder is for Granny Allen. She needs one to lift the kettle from the fire. I'm going to make another for Mother—and maybe one for Dilly, too."

Mary Ellen wrinkled her forehead with a worriment which had come to her. She wanted to send a present to all her folks on Far-Side. But how in the world could she do it? There were five children left at home besides her father and mother. Seven Christmas presents. There wouldn't be time to make a gift for everybody. And what could she make for the boys, anyway—for Big Abe, her eldest brother, for Ike and Jake, and little Tom Tad? Of course, Tom Tad was a baby and not so very hard to please. Cissie would like anything she made for her. And then, of course, there was Father. She might make him a handkerchief.

"What makes you sigh, Mary Ellen? Did you get a knot in your thread?" Lovie asked.

"No, the knot's in my head," was the answer, and she told Lovie her worriment. Lovie was an understanding person.

"I'll put my thinking cap on," she said. "Maybe I'll have a notion." But she didn't, that is, not right away.

One morning, a day or so later, she brought Mary Ellen a present to school, a little corn-shuck doll. She had made it the night before.

"My Mammy showed me how. Don't you think it is sort o' pretty?"

"A sight pretty!" Mary Ellen exclaimed. "Oh, Lovie, you are good to give me a present like this—and before Christmas, too!"

"Don't mention it," said the other, speaking in a

mannerly way. "I'm glad you like the shuck dolly."

"It's a sight pretty," Mary Ellen said again. And the doll was worthy of praises, with her smiling face painted with blackberry juice and her beautiful brown tresses made from curly corn silk. She had on a cap and apron and a little shawl with silky fringe. Yes, she was indeed a sight pretty, as Mary Ellen declared her to be.

That afternoon they were making Christmas presents when a lady came in. She was an outlander for certain, Mary Ellen saw as she entered the door. She knew it at once by her clothing and the way she said, "Good afternoon," instead of "Hello" or "Howdy."

Miss Ellison seemed to know her right away. She went to the door to meet her and, after a few minutes, brought her back to see what the school children were doing.

"Miss Andrews has come to visit our school," the teacher told the children. "She has come a long way—all the way from New York City."

"I remember that place," Lovie leaned over and whispered to Mary Ellen. "New York is pink in the Geography—like the bonnet I wore on Sunday last summer."

"'New York *City*,' she said, Lovie," Mary Ellen started explaining. "New York *City*'s a little black dot in the Geography." But now the outlander lady had come to stand at the end of their table. She was taking up the corn-shuck doll.

"Oh, that adorable dolly! I must have it for my collection at home. I have a hundred dolls," she added.

"I gathered them from all over the world during many years of travel."

"This doll is mine," Mary Ellen said. "Lovie gave it to me this morning. I reckon I couldn't give it away."

"Oh, no—I will buy it," said the lady. "You will let me buy it, won't you?" she asked.

But Mary Ellen looked troubled as she shook her head.

"Look!" the lady said. "I will give you this silver dollar. You can buy a lot of candy with it."

"Take the dollar, Mary Ellen," whispered Lovie. "I will make another doll for you."

"All right," agreed Mary Ellen, and the outlander lady laid the dollar in her hand. My, but it was a big piece of money! Still, she had a sort of lonesome feeling for her doll. She almost regretted her bargain as she saw her being carried away.

"What made you tell me to do it?" she asked Lovie with a tremble on her lips.

"Because I had a notion. It popped into my head all at once. Listen to me, Mary Ellen. Now you can buy Christmas presents. A dollar is a lot of money. It will buy presents for all your folks on the other side of the mountain."

"Oh," cried Mary Ellen. This joyful thought set up a carol within her. "Oh, Lovie, how good you are to have such a wonderful notion. That's what I'll do—that's what I'll do. And now, you will have to help me plan how to spend the money. It will take a sight of planning to spend a whole dollar, I reckon."

And it did. They went together down to the store after school was out and looked at the Christmas fixings on a special counter. On the other side of the mountain, Mary Ellen had never seen such a sight. There were tin horns and little red wagons, a monkey

Country store

which danced when you pulled a string, and a music box which played when its handle was turned. A sight to behold! Mary Ellen looked with wonder while she kept the dollar clutched in her hand, which was thrust deep in her pocket.

"How many presents will a dollar buy?" she asked the kind storekeeper, who waited on them patiently.

He smiled and waited half a minute before he answered.

"Well, it depends. Nearly all these things are a quarter apiece, you see."

"Then it wouldn't go around." Mary Ellen knew her multiplication tables well enough to figure that out. And she had to spend the dollar so that it would go around. It seemed now a much harder problem than any in her arithmetic.

"Look, Mary Ellen!" Lovie whispered. She pointed with an eager finger to a glass showcase that was nearly filled with striped peppermint candy.

"A dollar's worth of candy would be a whole lot," Lovie wisely suggested. "A dollar's worth of candy *would* go around and treat all your folks, Mary Ellen."

"Yes, it would!" Mary Ellen saw all at once a happy answer to her problem. A Christmas treat! They would all like that, from Father to the baby.

"Well, have you made up your mind?" asked the storekeeper. He was a very kind person and a patient one, but other customers were having to wait for him.

"Yes, sir," Mary Ellen replied. "A dollar's worth of peppermint candy."

And she and Lovie had a stick apiece as they walked up the mountain together.

10

Something for Dilly

Brother Martin stopped at Granny Allen's to tell her and Mary Ellen that they were invited to a housewarming on New Year's Day.

"A housewarming!" cried Granny Allen. "If there's any new house on this mountain, at least on Near-Side, I've heard no tell of it. Where might this house-warming be?"

Brother Martin's grave eyes twinkled a bit, and Mary Ellen wondered what funny notions he had in his head.

"I'll give you three guesses," he said, smiling at them broadly now, "and that is more than a plenty. I reckon you'll guess the house quick enough when I spill you a piece of news. Your granddaughter Dilly, Mary Ellen's sister, who got married last Christmas and has been living on Shoulder Blade, has moved to Near-Side—going to be neighbors."

"Well, that *is* news!" Granny Allen cried. "It does me good to hear it! Whereabouts on Near-Side, did you say?"

"In No-End Hollow," Brother Martin replied. "Nate got a job working in the timber on Near-Side. They're going to live here for sure enough, they say."

"Well and good," remarked Granny, nodding her head in a well-pleased fashion.

"Goody, goody!" Mary Ellen cried. If Dilly wasn't so far off, she could go and visit her every once in a while. She hadn't gone to the wedding last year—and hadn't seen Dilly since she married and moved away.

And now Granny Allen was saying, "We missed the wedding last year, but we won't miss this. My rheumatism is better, praise the Lord! And we'll be there as certain sure as Sunday!"

"Spread the news about a bit," advised Brother Martin. "Sound it all up and down the creek. I'll tell the folks on the way to Grassy Fork where I go to hold a meeting over Sunday. We'll get up a crowd that is a crowd. It will be more fun that way, and more help to the young folks."

"Yes, it will," agreed Granny Allen. "Never fear. We'll carry the news around."

Then the Circuit Rider rode away down Near-Side trail.

After he was gone, Granny Allen fell to planning what she should take for a housewarming gift.

"What in the world do I have, I wonder, that is fitting to give away?"

"And what do *I* have?" wondered Mary Ellen. She had just been thinking that she wanted to take a gift herself. Granny was now talking more to herself than to Mary Ellen.

"I could take her something from the cellar: apple

butter or huckleberry jam. We could spare that anyway, but she's certain sure to have a lot of such gifts. I'd like to take something special, seeing we are kinfolks."

"And so should I," echoed Mary Ellen.

"Well," Granny said, "it isn't today that we're going to the housewarming. We've got time to think about it, and I reckon we won't have to go empty-handed when the time comes to go."

Then she said Mary Ellen must go tell the news to Uncle Tobe Carr and Aunt Hannah who lived up the mountain a little ways. Mary Ellen was glad to go, for these near neighbors seemed like real kin.

She found both the old folks busy. Aunt Hannah was making ginger cakes. Uncle Tobe was sitting by the fire whittling away on a big gourd. Mary Ellen told her story and then sat down to eat a ginger cake and watch Uncle Tobe work awhile.

"I'll take a couple of goose-feather pillows," announced Aunt Hannah. "I have two that I can spare."

Uncle Tobe whittled away, making the round hole in the gourd bigger and bigger.

"I'll take a new ax handle I made just the other day."

"What's your granny taking?" Aunt Hannah asked.

Mary Ellen twisted a bit in the hickory splint chair. She did not know what to say, and yet she had to make some reply.

"Something—something good, I reckon," she answered as cheerfully as she could.

Aunt Hannah laughed and nodded. Then she gave

the little girl another cake.

"Oh, these are so good," Mary Ellen said, and she thanked her in a mannerly way. "Do you mind if I take this one to Granny? Granny hardly ever makes cookies."

"Of course not," Aunt Hannah replied. "But if you'll eat that one right away, I'll give you a plateful to take its place, and those will be for your granny."

Mary Ellen laughed. "Oh, Granny will be pleased."

Uncle Tobe was whittling away, very gently now. He turned the gourd over and over, looking to see if his work was all right.

"It'll do, I reckon," was his verdict.

"Oh, a little bowl!" Mary Ellen exclaimed. The old man handed it to her.

"Yes, it's a makeshift bowl, all right. We broke the sugar bowl this morning, and this will have to do till we get a better one."

"It's a nice brown," declared Mary Ellen, "but pretty large for a sugar bowl, I think."

"Too big," agreed Aunt Hannah. "I told him that."

"It's too big," said Uncle Tobe, "but I had no gourd that was little enough to make a right-sized sugar bowl."

"I have one!" cried Mary Ellen. "I have two or three that I found last fall. I'll bring you one," she promised.

"Do you want to swap with me?" Uncle Tobe asked.

Mary Ellen nodded, smiling, and Uncle Tobe gave her this bowl to keep. He whittled out a little cover to fit like a lid on top of the bowl.

"Now it's ready to take home," he told her.

"Not quite," Aunt Hannah said, and she took it and filled it with ginger cookies.

On her way home, Mary Ellen had a happy thought. She could take this gourd dish to Dilly. Uncle Tobe wouldn't mind. And when she talked it over with Granny, the old woman nodded her head.

"Yes, you can take the bowl to Dilly for a housewarming gift. It's a pretty fine bowl, and she'll find good use for it, I reckon." Then Granny had a notion all at once.

"I tell you, Mary Ellen! I'll give a bowl, too, my china sugar bowl! If Uncle Tobe and Aunt Hannah can make out with a sugar gourd, we can do it ourselves, I reckon, and so we'll get him to make us one."

"Oh, goody!" sang Mary Ellen.

The matter was settled for good and all. They could go to Dilly's housewarming with as high heads as anyone, for they wouldn't go empty-handed.

"Oh, goody!" she sang out again. Then she opened the ginger cookies. Granny Allen took one, and she took one. The rest they kept for Dilly.

11

The Housewarming

Mary Ellen wiggled deeper in the featherbed and buried her head in the pillow. The tip of her nose could tell right away that it was a very cold morning. Or was it morning? Yes, it must be. She could hear their old rooster crowing and then a distant cock-a-doodle from Uncle Tobe's higher up in the mountain. Listening, Mary Ellen slowly woke up enough to turn her head gently, and she caught a gray glimmer through the door-hinge chink. The window shutters were barred safely against strong winds these winter nights. But now it was surely morning. Then she had a quick, all-of-a-sudden thought. Why, this was New Year's morning! New Year's Day and a wonderful day for what was going to happen. She and Granny were going a-visiting. They were going to see Sister Dilly, who was having a housewarming that day in her new house in No-End Hollow. How good it would be to see her again after the long separation. Maybe she had grown so much that Dilly wouldn't know her!

She jumped up. No staying in bed; no dozing for her any longer. She was too excited to lie still, and she

thought she might as well get busy and have the fire
going when Granny woke up.

On the hearth she uncovered the embers carefully
bedded the night before. Then, with a handful of fine
splinters and a good breath or two, she had a blaze. A
new backlog was not needed, for the old one was not yet
burned up. She managed a fire stick neatly and piled on
plenty of smaller wood. The flames caught and crackled
in the chimney, warming the hearthstones with quick
heat. Mary Ellen felt chilly no longer as she dressed
before the fire, turning round and round.

"Sakes alive!" It was Granny Allen stirring in the
depths of her four-poster bed. "What makes you so
smart, Mary Ellen?"

"It's New Year's! It's New Year's!" Mary Ellen cried.
"Today we are going to Dilly's. Let's get an early start,
Granny!" she begged.

"We'll have to start early," answered Granny, "if we
want to get there and back inside of one day. Day doesn't
tarry long in these mountains this time o' year."

Mary Ellen asked, "Is it far down to No-End Hollow,
to where Dilly lives?"

"Yes, a right far piece," Granny Allen told her. "We'll
have to make fast tracks on our way."

Mary Ellen made herself handy helping get the
morning meal. They had hot corn mush that morning
with plenty of melted butter on it. A bit of hoe cake
left from supper was toasted brown before the fire and
eaten with a taste of molasses. After this, the house was

to be readied up, but this was all done in a hurry: dishes washed, beds made, and the floor swept clean. Then they dressed in their outdoor clothing, wrapping themselves up as warmly as they could. Granny wore her go-to-meeting shawl and bonnet in honor of the grand to-do. In the mountains, a housewarming is a very important affair indeed. Then it is that all of the neighbors carry to a newly-wedded pair the gifts they know will be needed to help them in starting to keep house. Mary Ellen was happy in thinking that both she and Granny had a gift to take along. And how pleased and surprised would Dilly be to have her granny's china sugar bowl and her gourd full of ginger cookies!

At the last moment, Granny dropped two hot potatoes into Mary Ellen's coat pockets.

"To warm your fingers on, child," she said. "And when you get hungry, you can eat 'em."

As they started down the trail, they looked up the mountain to see if any neighbors were coming their way, but they saw no sign of anybody.

"Uncle Tobe and Aunt Hannah are sure to come. They promised," said Mary Ellen. She had hoped to have them for company.

"They'll be along later," said Granny. "But I reckon they'll ride in the one-horse cart. We had better just keep on walking. Maybe they will overtake us by and by."

On account of her rheumatism, Granny had to take her time on the trail, and she came after Mary Ellen, who ran ahead with hops and skips till she got so far ahead of Granny that she had to wait for her to catch up.

The trail curled around the mountain and after a time entered No-End Hollow. Here it was indeed rough going, for it followed the edge of a creek bed. Sometimes they had to cross the water of the twisting, turning creek itself, and this they did by picking out stepping stones to the other side. At last Granny felt so weary that she sat down to rest before they went on. Mary Ellen sat down beside her and ate a potato. She offered Granny one, but the old woman said she was not hungry.

"I just want to rest my bones a bit," she said as she turned her shoulders to catch the warmth of the morning sun that had now climbed over the mountain till the hollow had a peep of it.

Up the creek they heard a splashing and a great creaking of wagon wheels.

"It's Uncle Tobe and Aunt Hannah!" Mary Ellen cried as they came into view. And indeed it was their neighbors, catching up with them at last.

They stopped and invited Granny to get into the cart, but she said, "There isn't room enough for me."

"You may have my place," Uncle Tobe told her. "You can sit up here with Hannah. She knows how to drive as well as I do, and I'll walk along with Mary Ellen."

To this the old woman at last agreed, and it was a blessing to her to be picked up in this way.

"I feel tuckered out," she acknowledged.

At Dilly's house they found a great stir. Already so many people had gathered from Near-Side-And-Far that the house itself couldn't hold them. A big fire had been built in the yard, and around this the neighbor folk gathered to talk to one another and have a big time.

Mary Ellen ran straight to Dilly and put her gift into her hand.

"Dilly! Dilly! Do you know me?" And she threw her arms around her sister.

Dilly hugged and kissed her. "Why, of course, goosy!" she said, almost crying. "What makes you say that—did you think I wouldn't know you?"

"Well—I was afraid—I've grown up so much since I saw you," Mary Ellen replied.

Dilly laughed and hugged her again. Then she examined her present.

"Well, if that isn't a pretty now. I declare it is! I am much obliged to you, honey."

Then her husband, good-looking Nate Turner, came up and shook hands with Mary Ellen. He stole a handful of cookies from the gourd which Dilly had set down, winking slyly at Mary Ellen.

"Don't tell on me now, will you?" he begged.

Mary Ellen laughed as she answered, "Half of them are yours by right, I reckon, but you must save the other half for Dilly."

Dilly bore Mary Ellen off to see the other things which the neighbors had brought her. These were in the living room of the double log house. There were a great many presents: a new featherbed, a stack of quilts, two pillows—these were from Aunt Hannah—a shuck boot mat to lay at the door, a new broom, a bench, and a table. These were some of the things that Mary Ellen saw at once. Of course, there were many others. A row of jars sat on the mantel shelf—preserves and jams and jellies. In a kitchen corner was a bag of new meal, and above it from a rafter was hung a good-sized and well cured ham.

When it was time for dinner, the men made up the big open fire, and the women brought pans and kettles and heated up the food that they had brought. Mary Ellen and the other children had to watch things so that they would not burn. Just as they were serving the dinner on scantling tables around the fire, who should come but Brother Martin, in the nick of time, to ask a blessing on the food and to shake hands with everybody. Such a fine feast it was, too, Mary Ellen thought. And there was such aplenty of the good things, too. She had two helpings of chicken, dumplings, and gravy and two pieces of stack cake.

As soon as dinner was over, Brother Martin made a little talk. It wasn't an ordinary sermon like the ones he preached in the meetinghouse. He talked about Nate and Dilly and their nice new home. He wished them all well, and there was more handshaking among the crowd just to show that the neighbors agreed with these good wishes.

"Let's have a play party!" somebody cried when all the handshaking was over.

A play party was a sight of fun, and even the Circuit

Rider had no word to say against it when held in a seemly manner.

"Bring out the fiddles first!" someone called. It seemed there were several ready, for they appeared without delay. They struck up a ballad tune, and everybody who knew it helped sing the words of "Barbara Allen."

> *"In Salem town where I was born,*
> *There was a fair maid dwelling,*
> *Made every youth cry, 'Well-a-day!'*
> *Her name was Barbara Allen."*

In Salem town where I was born, there was a fair maid dwelling,

Made every youth cry, "Well-a-day!" Her name was Barbara Allen.

There was more of it, a great deal more—in all, nineteen verses, and Mary Ellen knew most of them. Then they sang a ballad called "Lord Thomas" and another called "The Golden Vanity." Then the younger folks started playing the games they liked best, "London Bridge," "Go Round and Round the Village," "The Dusty Miller," and "Skip to My Lou."

Mary Ellen was glad that Dilly played all the games as she used to do, just as if she were not married and settled down like grown-up folks.

"A penny for your thoughts, Mary Ellen," Uncle Tobe said on the way home. Mary Ellen was walking beside him. Aunt Hannah and Granny were ahead in the cart.

"A penny for your thoughts, Mary Ellen," he said again. Mary Ellen looked up.

"I was thinking that I'll have a housewarming myself someday, and I'll invite you and Aunt Hannah and everybody else who was there today."

"Much obliged, honey," Uncle Tobe thanked her, speaking in his usual mannerly way, and he felt in his pocket for a penny.

12

The Scarecrow

Winter passed slowly from Near-Side-And-Far, and spring, when it came, was welcome. First, Mary Ellen found some tiny blue flowers under a limestone ledge. She took these to school and learned their name, hepaticas, from the teacher. A little later there was trailing arbutus under the big pine trees.

How good it was to open the house to the first mild breezes, to swing wide the window shutters and let the sunshine in!

When the green leaves of the hickory trees were about as big as a squirrel's ears, they planted their garden and a corn patch. Granny Allen's rheumatism was better now, as it always was in the springtime of the year. She threw away her walking stick and leaned on a hoe handle. Mary Ellen worked with her, and Granny declared she could do as well as anyone twice her size and a good deal older.

It was too bad that she had to miss school to help with the corn planting, but she couldn't let Granny do all the hard work alone. She would study hard when she got back and make up her lessons.

And that's what she did. But more trouble came on

later. While they were planting their second patch of corn, the first came up, and the crows began to pull it up. Then somebody had to stay on watch to guard it from the thieves.

One day Mary Ellen sat on a stump in the middle of the new-ground corn patch and listened to a crow's protesting "Cawl" in a pine on the edge of the clearing

"He sees me here," thought Mary Ellen. "I guess he is telling the others that they'll have to wait till I go away—the mean old robbers!"

For three days now, she had been obliged to stay out here in the corn patch and guard the sprouting grain from the crows. They had already done much damage here when Granny Allen had discovered the thieves. She was greatly distressed about it. The new-ground field had been prepared at the cost of much time and hard labor. She and Mary Ellen had dug up sprouts, briers, and weeds and burned them. They had also cleared the land of stones.

Uncle Tobe, their nearest neighbor, had plowed the ground and helped them plant it. They were hoping to gather in the autumn enough corn to last all winter. But now the crows had found it and threatened to gobble up the whole crop before it was fairly started.

And this wasn't all—though it was bad enough. Granny Allen was going to the Mission with fresh eggs for Miss Ellison. It had been a week since she had seen her, so of course she wanted to go along with Granny and explain that she'd had to stay out of school to help

"For three days she had been obliged to guard the sprouting
grains from the crows"

plant corn and guard what was coming up. Of course, Granny could do the explaining, but—well, Mary Ellen was tired of staying home.

"What's the matter with you, Mary Ellen?" It was Uncle Tobe coming up behind her. "You look all hunched up there on that stump like you had a misery in you."

Mary Ellen smiled up at Uncle Tobe and explained the "misery" within her.

"Hmm, that's too bad now," Uncle Tobe said, sympathetic. "Reckon you're all worn out anyway settin' there in this corn patch keepin' that pesky lot o' thieves away."

"Oh, I *am*," said Mary Ellen, "but I wouldn't mind sitting out here by myself—though I do get pretty lonesome—if I could go to the Mission with Granny."

She sighed, and Uncle Tobe nodded. "I wish I could stay in your place," he said, "but I've got to do some plowin'. I'd make a good scarecrow," he added with a chuckle, looking at his ragged garments.

"A scarecrow!" Mary Ellen exclaimed. Why hadn't she thought of it sooner? She and Granny had made a scarecrow once to keep the hawks off the baby chickens.

"I know how to make a scarecrow," she said. "I believe I'll make one, Uncle Tobe, and try it out. If it keeps the crows away, I can go along with Granny."

"Better make it to look as much like you as you can," advised Uncle Tobe. "Crow birds are mighty smart critters, they say, and it takes a good scarecrow to fool 'em."

"Well," said Mary Ellen with a laugh, "Granny often says I look like a scarecrow the way I run around sometimes, so maybe it will be easy to make a scarecrow look like me! Listen, Uncle Tobe, I have an idea. I believe I can make a scarecrow right here. I can spare this shawl and apron—my sunbonnet, too. Wouldn't that be enough? But I'll have to get a frame made somehow. Just two sticks—that's all I need—one long one, for the body, and one a little shorter for the outstretched arms."

"I'll make you one," offered Uncle Tobe. "There's some poles left from a brush-pile fire I noticed a little way back yonder."

She went to get the sticks and was soon back. With a stout string, he bound them together.

"Now to dress it up," said Mary Ellen. She first tied her blue-checked apron about the long pole so that it would look as much like a dress skirt as possible. Around the crosspiece arms she draped the shawl. On top she hung her old sunbonnet.

"It *does* look a lot like me," she said and couldn't keep back a giggle as Uncle Tobe set it up in the ground.

"Now let's slip away and hide a few minutes behind those trees," the old man suggested. "We can watch from there and see if it works."

Not long afterward a lone crow left the woods and flew over the cornfield. He flew in a circle above the scarecrow—but very high above it.

"Sort of curious," said Uncle Tobe. "Maybe he's a little mite suspicious—but he means to play it safe."

The crow flew away. Later on, they heard a distant caw-cawing, as if a flock of crows were engaged in an excited conversation. Minutes passed—no crows returned. They stayed and watched a while longer. Still no crows.

"I reckon that scarecrow has scared 'em all right," said Uncle Tobe. "You run along and got ready to go to the Mission with your granny."

Maybe—oh, maybe the scarecrow could guard the corn, thought Mary Ellen, so that she could go back to school. That would be good news for certain! Almost too good to be true!

"Oh," said Mary Ellen, "do you think it will be safe? I couldn't bear to come back later and find that the crows had been into our corn. Perhaps I had better not risk it."

"I don't think you need to worry a mite—not a mite," replied Uncle Tobe. "That's a good scarecrow. But I'll tell you something else to make your mind rest easy. I'll plow the part of my field that's next to this while you are gone to the Mission. And then I can keep an eye on things. You tell that to your granny when you're telling about the scarecrow. It will make her better satisfied and more agreeable to have you go along."

"Uncle Tobe, you are the kindest person! I don't know how to thank you," Mary Ellen said.

"Don't mention it," Uncle Tobe answered. "I'm always glad to do a favor. And you and Granny are good neighbors."

Mary Ellen had another thought. She had a sudden

thought of a good way to reward Uncle Tobe.

"Uncle Tobe, I'm going to get a new book to read while I'm at the Mission. The name of it is *Gulliver's Travels*, and if you like, I will read it to you."

"I'd like that fine, Mary Ellen," Uncle Tobe said heartily. Like Granny Allen, he could not read for himself, so this would give him real pleasure.

As Mary Ellen slipped between the rows of corn on her way to the cabin, these words rang in her mind, "You and Granny are good neighbors." Well, she would try to keep on being one. It really wasn't very hard to do.

The scarecrow proved to be a faithful guard. The crows forsook the cornfield after it was set up. Mary Ellen went back to school again. And to repay Uncle Tobe, Mary Ellen read him *Gulliver's Travels* off and on till she got to the end.

13

High Water

The Mission school closed in May that year. This was always a great occasion, when fathers, mothers, and neighbor folk came to hear the children speak and sing. Everyone who could chirp a note or remember two lines that went together made his bow to the public this day. And it was a notable thing to make a lengthy recitation. A piece that had many verses won cheers that were both long and loud, and the pupil who could sing "Lord Thomas" or "Fair Ellender" or "The Ballad of Barbara Allen" was certain of violent applause.

Speeches were cut from the aged magazines or the old newspapers which occasionally found a wandering way into a home of Near-Side. Another and more convenient source of supply was the *Language* and the *Reader* and even the red-backed *Spelling Book* with a verse at the foot of each page.

Those who liked easy and short pieces picked theirs out of the speller. Those who were a little more ambitious thumbed a reader's page. But for the ones whose aspirations looked still higher, there was the "Appendix" of the *Language*. Here there were many pages of both prose and poetry, a miscellaneous collection. From these selections, one picked out, day after day, the parts of speech.

Gray's "Elegy" with its thirty-two verses was the last. It took six pages of the book. Mary Ellen remembered the day when the daring thought had flashed into her mind:

"I should like to learn that poem. What a nice long piece it would make to say in school someday!"

And she had learned it! She knew it all now. She had learned it little by little, at odd times now and then, with the book upon her knee as she churned out on the dogtrot early in the morning, or while she waited for the kettle to boil or the bread to brown. She had begun to learn it long ago—it was away back last fall. And now it was spring on the mountain again and time for school closing again.

"What speech are you going to say the last day of school?" all the children kept asking her. But Mary Ellen would not tell them.

"You'll be surprised when you find out," was all that she would say. And wouldn't they be surprised, she thought. They had never heard the "Elegy" given as a recitation. She was very certain sure of that. She was ready for the last day.

This was more than could be said of some of the other children. Poor Lovie Lane was always behind when she had a speech to say. She started to learn several but became discouraged with them and kept trying to find something easier. So it was that time slipped away, and only three days were left. She told Mary Ellen her troubles.

"What shall I do? What shall I do? I can't get up and say a line of this and a line of that—and that's all I know!" She was tearful as she thought of it.

Mary Ellen put her thinking cap on.

"Could you learn a verse a day for three days?" she asked her friend.

"Oh, I think—yes, I'm sure I could," said Lovie.

"Then I'll share my speech with you," Mary Ellen told her. The secret must be told, but no matter. The last three verses—"The Epitaph"—this was the part Lovie could say, and if she forgot it when she got up, as sometimes happened, why it would be easy to whisper a word and start her right again.

The night before the closing day of school, a rainstorm fell on the mountain. A fearful storm it was, too. It had been many a day since the folk on Near-Side had seen so much water rushing down No-End Creek. It bore large trees away as if they had been broken twigs.

Mary Ellen stood with Granny Allen in the dogtrot and watched the flood.

"We are safe, I am thankful to say," declared Granny Allen. And, of course, Mary Ellen was thankful, too, but a sad thought had come to her. The water was over the foot log, and how could she cross the creek to go to the Mission school today?

"Don't worry yet," advised Granny. "It's early and a long time till ten o'clock. The water may be low then."

School opened later on the last day to allow everybody on the mountain plenty of time to get there. Hour after hour slipped away. It was nine o'clock at last and time to go. But No-End Creek was still roaring, and the foot log was covered at least two feet.

Aunt Hannah and Uncle Tobe appeared. They always went to the Mission on any special occasion.

"Well, I reckon we'll have to stay on this side," Aunt Hannah declared.

"Oh, oh!" wailed Mary Ellen. "I won't get to say the 'Elegy,' and Lovie will be too scared to say *The Epitaph* all by herself!" She was very close to crying with vexation and disappointment.

"Too bad, honey," Granny said.

"Too bad," Uncle Tobe echoed. "It would take a boat to get us across."

Mary Ellen ran away to cry to herself behind the house, and then she kept on going till she got to the barn lot. She thought it was better for her to get clear away while she was going. She might cry aloud and behave just like a baby when once she started. She felt just as if she had a flood inside her that was tearing along like the waters of the creek sweeping down No-End Hollow.

She leaned against the watering trough and cried fully for five minutes. After that she felt much better, and then she washed the tears from her face in the clear rain water of the trough. The trough was a big log hollowed deep enough to hold water for stock. It looked a lot like a canoe. Mary Ellen thought of this all of a sudden, and the next minute she was tearing back to the house.

"Uncle Tobe! Uncle Tobe! Will the watering trough do?"

"Do?" said Uncle Tobe, mystified.

"Do for a boat!" Mary Ellen was jumping up and down before him. Light dawned on Uncle Tobe.

"I declare upon my honor," he shouted, "that's a wonderful idea." And with Mary Ellen in the lead, they ran to the barn.

Everybody was needed, too, even Granny Allen, who helped roll the old trough downhill. At last they made the final turn, and it lay at the edge of No-End Creek.

Now to try it in the water! Uncle Tobe cut a long, stout, smooth pole to use in guiding it over. He went across the creek and back again to show them it could be done. Then, one by one, he took them all over: Granny Allen, then Aunt Hannah, and last of all, Mary Ellen. It was a great deal of fun riding across in the water-trough boat, and it went over sure and steady under Uncle Tobe's careful hand.

They were almost the last ones to get to the schoolhouse, and the speaking, as they saw, was already beginning. Mary Ellen saw Lovie waving at her and went up to sit by her.

"What made you so late?" Lovie asked. But Mary Ellen shook her head at her. "I'll tell you later—it's a long tale." Then she remembered something, "Don't forget 'Melancholy' in your second verse, Lovie. Try to say it right this time."

And then the teacher was reading their names from the program, "Gray's 'Elegy in a Country Churchyard' by Mary Ellen Morrison and Lovie Lane."

There was a little rustle of stiffly starched dresses and bonnets and a chorus of creaks along the rows of school benches. Mary Ellen felt the eyes of the crowd upon them as they walked up to the platform. She was conscious of a squeak, squeak in her new shoes and tried to step as lightly as she could. All of a sudden now it seemed that her waistband pinched her. She wanted to throw back her shoulders and get a breath, a big breath, before she started to say Gray's "Elegy." Would she remember all of those thirty-two verses? She would have to keep up with Lovie, too, and help her if help were needed.

She glanced at her friend as they took their places by the teacher's desk on the platform. Lovie gave her a fleeting smile—she wasn't worried, not a bit, but then she hadn't much to worry about—only three short verses and somebody to remind her if she forgot any of it!

The people down below blurred for a moment like a crazy quilt of many colors. Then Mary Ellen saw Granny's little brown face smiling up at her pridefully. She must do her best for Granny. She found her tongue then and began:

> "The curfew tolls the knell of parting day,
> The lowing herds wind slowly o'er the lea;
> The plowman homeward plods his weary way,
> And leaves the world to darkness and to me."

She was in full swing now. It wasn't any trouble to remember a long speech if you could keep thinking of what came next. She got over the hard words like "grandeur," "heraldry," and "celestial" without tying her tongue in a knot. The teacher would be pleased after having pronounced them at least a dozen times for her.

And now she came to her favorite lincoi

"Full many a gem of purest ray serene
The dark unfathomed caves of ocean bear:
Full many a flower is born to blush unseen
And waste its sweetness on the desert air."

She heard Lovie sigh. Mary Ellen knew that she was thinking of having to stand there and wait until all the other fifteen verses were said.

As she went on, Mary Ellen saw Granny push back her sunbonnet and lean forward as if she were minded not to miss a word. Aunt Hannah beside her did the same, and Uncle Tobe put his hand up beside his head to catch the sense and sound in his one good ear. Mary Ellen raised her voice and went ahead. Everybody was paying good attention, even those on the back seats and the ones who stood around the door.

And now she had come to the end of her part, and she turned slightly to Lovie to warn her to begin.

"*The Epitaph!*" she whispered to her, as Lovie hesitated.

Lovie blinked a bit and began in singsong fashion the

lines which her friend had drilled her on.

"Here rests his head—" and she stuck fast in a helpless fashion. Mary Ellen whispered a word or two, and Lovie went on in a solemn, determined tone:

> "Here rests his head upon the lap of Earth,
> A Youth of Fortune and to Fame unknown.
> Fair—fair—fair——"

She faltered again.

"Science!" hissed Mary Ellen.

> "Fair science frowned not on his humble birth.
> And Melancholy marked him for her own."

Then she made a bow and started off the platform.

"You forgot—" Mary Ellen began, but she had no chance for saying the rest of what she had started to say, for Lovie was going ahead, and she was obliged to follow her. Oh, why had Lovie failed her and forgotten outright the last line of her speech?

But the crowd was cheering them—a regular hip-and-hurrah it was with all the hand clapping and stamping of feet. They had liked the speech anyway— and, of course, thought Mary Ellen, it was so long that nobody could guess that there was any left out of it!

"She found her tongue then and began"

14

A Morning on Piney Spur

May passed, and then June, and now it was summer. One could go barefoot again and wade in the creek these days. There were dewberries ripening along the fence corners, and on the south side of the mountains, early huckleberries were turning blue. After a week of rain, there came a hot spell, and they ripened fast. They were selling for twenty-five cents a gallon now at the Cross Roads store. Two gallons of berries would buy a new dress, a new calico dress for Sunday. Four gallons would buy a pair of shoes like the ones Lovie Lane had worn to meeting.

"Ninety-eight cents in the summer catalogue," her friend had confided to her. "Everything in it is down to half price."

They were white shoes with shiny buckles and much ornamental stitching. Pretty as a picture they were indeed, and Mary Ellen wanted some, too. Perhaps if the price of berries stayed up, and if she found good picking, she might make enough money for a new dress and even for new shoes! She had high hopes as she went along the trail one pleasant summer morning. It was early in the day, and the sun had not risen above Near-Side-And-Far. The trail was dewy, and the bracken fronds brushed her bare legs and dampened her skirt till it flapped wet against her knees. At long last, it was such a bother that she stopped and wrung the water out. It would dry out, she thought, a little later when she had climbed to a sunny place higher up on the side of the mountain.

She now saw a huckleberry bush that had a few ripe berries, and she picked a handful. She hurried on now more hopefully. Now the trail was getting steeper. After a minute she stopped to get her breath, and looking around beyond her, she saw her first good patch that day. How pretty were the bushes laden with the blue berry clusters, wet with dew and shining with the sun upon them till it was truly a sight to behold. Mary Ellen had an eye for beauty wherever she was and whatever she was doing when its loveliness came upon her.

"A right pretty sight," she thought now to herself. Then she bent above the bush nearest to her and began the task of filling up. Rattle—rattle—thud! The berries dropped merrily into her tin bucket, and soon she had the bottom covered. It wouldn't take very long to fill up in a fine patch like this, thought Mary Ellen. A blessed day it was for her. She lifted her head at the sound of the voices that seemed to come from somewhere down in the hollow on the other side of Piney Spur. Then a dog began barking, too.

"Here, Nap, here!" a boy's voice called, and a girl's

voice echoed, "Here, Nap!"

The Hackett twins! Jodie and Jobie were out after berries, too. She hadn't seen them since school was out last May.

"Hoo-hoo!" she called. They answered her, and as soon as they found who it was above them, they climbed on up the mountain.

"Whew! What a fine patch of berries!" Jobie cried.

"I'll say!" exclaimed his sister Jodie.

"Enough for us all, I guess," Mary Ellen said.

This meeting with the twins was welcome, for although they were younger than she, they were good company for Mary Ellen.

They were picking their berries to sell, too. And they got thirty-five cents a gallon at Turn-Off, a store beyond Cross Roads.

"But that's so far," objected Mary Ellen. "I never could carry my berries there."

"We haul 'em," was Jobie's explanation. "Everybody at our house is picking today except Grandmommy and the baby. Tomorrow, Matt'll take 'em to Turn-Off in the one-horse wagon."

"Oh," Mary Ellen sighed. "I wish—" but she stopped. She wouldn't say what she was thinking—that Matt could take her berries, too, for it might sound like hinting.

"Yip-yap!" They looked at Old Nap the dog who was leaping about in the bushes as if a booger was after him.

"It's a bee!" exclaimed Jobie, and he started out to help Nap, waving his rush hat madly this way and that.

"He started out to help Nap, waving his rush hat madly..."

"Look out!" called Mary Ellen, "you'll get stung yourself." And he did—right away. He tried to be brave about it, but he couldn't keep from crying, it hurt so badly.

"Let's go home," suggested his sister, distressed to see him rocking back and forth, nursing his swollen finger.

"Let's doctor it first," Mary Ellen said. She had had a bee sting last summer and remembered what her mother had done for it.

"A mud poultice is the very thing," she told him. "It's an Indian remedy, my mother said."

"Oh, that feels so good," said Jobie a few minutes later when the mud plaster was daubed on his throbbing finger. "It feels better all at once," he declared.

He seemed now to be in no hurry to set off for home. He sat down in the shade with Nap panting close beside him while the girls picked berries nearby.

Time passed. The sun above the mountain made small shadows now, Mary Ellen saw. It would be time for dinner when she could step on the shadow of her head. This was something that her brother had taught her. Well, she would soon be ready to go home. Her bucket was full already, and she had only to put on the heap. She saw that Jobie was sleeping beneath the pine, and Jodie was picking just a little way below her.

Jobie's bucket was, she saw as she peeped into it, hardly half-full, and she pondered on a generous thought that had come to her. Suppose she should fill it for him before he awoke? What a fine surprise that would be for him. She set down her own bucket, heaping full now, and began to pick into Jobie's. It wouldn't take very long if she picked away in a hurry.

"Hall-oo-oo!" a long-drawn call came from

somewhere down the hollow. Nap leaped up and bounded away.

"That's Matt, I reckon," said Jodie. "Hall-oo-oo!" she called to answer him. "He wants to know where we are," she added.

It was a little while later that Matt himself climbed into view.

"Time to mosey on down the mountain," he told his little sister. Then, "Howdy!" he said, as he caught sight of Mary Ellen.

"Where's Jobie?" he asked.

Jobie answered for himself, for by this time he had been awakened, and he came out to tell his woeful tale and to show his bee-stung finger.

"But it doesn't hurt me *half* as bad as it did. Mary Ellen doctored it," he told his brother.

"Say 'much obliged' to her," his big brother said, "and we've got to trail down the mountain."

Jobie looked for his bucket and found it pretty close to the place where he had left it.

"But I never picked it full!" he cried, looking all around. "Was it you?" he asked of his sister. Jodie shook her head.

"Well, then it was *you*, Mary Ellen! I am much obliged to you for that, too. She's a fine berry picker," he added, "but she doesn't get as much as we do—just twenty-five cents a gallon."

"Is that so?" Matt asked. And then, all at once, Matt had a very fine notion.

"You let me sell these berries for you. It won't be a bit of trouble, and if you pick more, I can sell them, too."

"I'm mighty much obliged," said Mary Ellen. "It would be a kind and neighborly turn."

"One good turn deserves another," Matt quoted, "and you have done *two* good turns. But I reckon we'll manage to get even."

Mary Ellen thought going home that day: "It's going to be a good summer. Summer—summer!" She skipped to the tune that her heart began to sing.

The End

More Books from The Good and the Beautiful Library

Boy of the Pyramids
by
Ruth Fosdick Jones

Mr. Apple's Family
by
Jean McDevitt

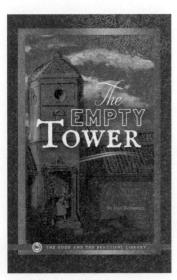

The Empty Tower
by
Jean Bothwell

Girl with a Musket
by
Florence Parker Simister